LILY ROSE

CD Gray

Dedication

I would like to Dedicate this to

Ellie and Clayton and to the

Memory of Suzanne...Forever Beautiful,

strong and courageous. We will Always love you and miss you.

Contents

Chapter 1
The Making of Lily Rose

It was a beautiful summer day in Dublin, Ireland. Eighteen-year-old Lily Rose had just entered the Irish Military Academy, a moment she had waited for her whole life. She had big dreams. After two years of Cadet Training at the Academy, she planned to attend Officers Training and then join the Irish Special Forces.

Lily Rose was a real beauty: long black hair, big dark brown eyes, an olive complexion, and tanned skin. She was the oldest child of Harry and Shelly. Harry was a skilled tradesman, and Shelly worked for a doctor in town. They had worked hard their whole lives to provide a good life for their children. Lily Rose had a younger brother and two younger sisters who looked up to her, and she knew she had to be a good example for them.

Not only did she excel in her learning, but she also mastered the art of Karate, earning a third-degree black belt. Lily Rose lived life her way—on her terms—but she was also very disciplined. She knew what she wanted and worked hard to achieve it. Kind and caring, yet willing to wreak havoc on anyone who threatened her, she had friends growing up but preferred being a loner.

And so, off to the Academy she went. Today marked the first day of the rest of her life, and she was ready. She said her goodbyes to her family, climbed onto the bus, and just like that… she was gone.

Time passed quickly. One month led to another, and one year after the next, until Lily Rose, now 25, had not only completed her Academy training but had also finished her Officers Training. Now, she was off to her goal: Special Forces training.

She was the only female who had what it took to compete with the men. She was next in line to face Captain Chris De Luca, a Special Forces Captain in the United States Marine Corps and a 5th-degree black belt, sent to Ireland to help train the newest cadets in the Irish Special Forces.

The boxing ring was set, and one by one, the cadets fell during their Karate skills training. Lily Rose sat quietly, observing, her mind slipping back to the age of 18, training with her Sensei.

Lily Rose stood blindfolded, patiently waiting for her Sensei to begin. Then, suddenly, her Sensei attacked. She fought back, every move a memory of years of Karate training. She held her own as her Sensei came at her with everything he had. Suddenly, she spun and kicked, but as she tumbled to the ground, her Sensei knocked her down with a powerful kick.

As she stood up, he removed her blindfold and scolded her. "You must never lose your focus, Lily Rose! Always anticipate the enemy's next move!"

Just then, Captain Chris De Luca called her name. "Lily Rose! You're up!"

For a moment, she lost her focus, but quickly regained it. She approached the ring and bowed to her opponent. Captain De Luca half-smiled and bowed in return. Without hesitation, Lily Rose launched herself at him with everything she had. She was fast— really fast. She spun and kicked, knocking him to the floor. Her classmates from the Special Forces Officers' class cheered. None of them had been able to get past Captain De Luca. He had beaten them all… until now. At just five feet three inches, Lily Rose was mighty.

Captain De Luca wiped the blood from the side of his mouth, surprised at her skill. He had planned on going easy on her because she was a woman, but he knew better now. They stared at each other intensely before the battle resumed. Hand to hand, they fought. He spun and kicked but missed her. Lily Rose was much too fast. Anger flashed in his eyes as he clenched his jaw.

Then, with one quick move, he flipped her over and pinned her to the ground. He thought he had her, but Lily Rose used her legs to scissor his head and squeezed. She lifted herself off the ground and quickly pinned him to the floor. Their eyes locked—his deep blue eyes meeting her dark brown eyes.

Then, the whistle blew. The referee called it a tie.

As they both stood up, Captain De Luca shook her hand,

saying, "Good job!" He realized how small and soft her hand was. Lily Rose smiled and left, though she was moved by his intense gaze. They had connected on a level she had never known before.

That night, as Lily Rose slept, she smiled to herself, remembering Captain De Luca's deep blue eyes.

Time flew, and soon it was graduation day. The officers had finally become part of the Irish Special Forces and were assigned special tasks. Lily Rose was shocked when she saw hers. She had been requested by the United States Marine Corps to assist in an undercover operation in Venezuela. Her jaw dropped. There was no time to waste. Her plane was leaving that night. She spent the day saying her goodbyes, packed, and was off to her new adventure as Agent #79, AKA Maria Vasquez.

Chapter 2
The Assignment

Her plane arrived on a hot, sunny day just west of Venezuela, close to the border of Colombia. Her assignment was to infiltrate and stop the arms trade between Venezuela and Colombia. Lily Rose met her good friend Gabrielle after she onboarded her plane and settled into her hotel. They met for cocktails at a nearby restaurant. Along with Gabrielle was her boyfriend, John Cruise—a tall, dashing man. He had dark hair and eyes to match. She quickly introduced Lily Rose to him. There was something about him that unsettled Lily. He seemed overly confident. Gabrielle and Lily Rose hugged and talked all night, catching up on the last several years.

The next day, they went for a swim at the beach. They made a day of sun and surf—two beautiful women that were total opposites. Gabrielle was a tall blonde with bouncy curls and pale white skin. They had met in grammar school and had been friends ever since. Gabrielle was a schoolteacher and had moved to Venezuela several years ago to help the country's poorest children. She was very kind and caring and completely unaware of why Lily Rose had been sent there.

After going for a quick swim, Lily Rose came out of the water. The sun glistened over her tanned body. Her long, black hair clung to her wet body, and her straight, white teeth shone brightly as she smiled. She had a toned body that ached to be kissed. She was a real beauty.

As she reached down on the white sand for her towel, a man she hadn't met—yet knew very well—walked up beside her and handed her a towel. It was the notorious Alexander Perez. Lily Rose knew him instantly. She had been prepared by the USMC before her mission, and one of the pictures given to her was of Alexander. He had a rap sheet a mile long. He was a paid assistant to the notorious General Nicolas Matias of Colombia. General Matias, along with General Alfredo Hernandez of Venezuela, were the two main people that Lily Rose was after for illegal arms trade, with the help of Vladimir Putchenski of Russia. The President was paying the two generals to funnel arms from the Middle East to his country, Russia.

"Hello! I am Alexander Perez."

"I was having lunch at the restaurant and couldn't help but admire your beauty."

Lily Rose quickly put on her game face and responded with charm and grace.

"Hello! I'm Maria," she said with a sweet smile.

"I was wondering if you would like to join me for lunch?" Alexander asked.

"Well, I have my friend with me right now," she replied.

"Bring her with you!" he quickly said.

Lily Rose turned and said, "Give me just a moment."

She proceeded to walk over to Gabrielle, and as they talked, he gazed at them both. Then, after only a minute or two, Lily Rose returned.

"She has some work to do, but I'll be glad to join you," Lily Rose said sweetly.

They turned and left. As they made their way up the beach to the restaurant, he gently put his hand on the small of her back as they began to talk.

As Alexander and Maria ate lunch, she seemed to charm her way through their conversation. He smiled at her as he noticed how the sun gleamed over her tanned skin and made her long, black hair glisten. By the end of lunch, Alexander was quite smitten with Maria. He decided that he was going to ask her to the dinner party that was only for the elite of Venezuela. Every big name would be in attendance. He looked into her big, brown eyes and said, "Miss Maria, there is going to be a very elegant dinner party tonight at the Chalise Hotel. Everyone of rank and stature will be there. Would you please do me the honor and be my date?"

Lily Rose was thinking how easy this had been so far. She

had somehow gotten the attention of General Nicolas Matias's closest man. She quickly smiled as she said, "I would be delighted to go with you tonight."

He smiled as he picked up her small hand and gently kissed it.

"Tonight, then, my beautiful Maria."

Alexander quickly paid the bill, and before he left, Lily Rose noticed that he had laid a one-hundred-dollar bill on the table as a tip.

Chapter 3

The Dinner Party

Alexander arrived that night at approximately eight o'clock. He knocked on her hotel door, and as the door opened, the vision that stood before him took his breath away.

Lily Rose was wearing a long, black evening gown. It was tight-fitting, and the front was low cut, exposing her large, round breasts, but it also revealed her slim back. She also had three-inch heels on that matched perfectly with her dress. Her long, black hair was swept up off her shoulders and twisted on top of her head, with only tiny wisps of hair falling against her face. Her jewelry was modest. Her beautiful white teeth shone brightly against her full ruby red lips. Alexander's jaw dropped as he smiled and said, "You look stunning, Maria!"

He locked her arm in his, and they quickly made their way to the limo that was waiting for them downstairs. They soon arrived at the dinner party. Lily Rose couldn't believe all the flashing lights and cameras. They made their way up the red carpet, and Lily Rose couldn't help but notice all the beautiful women wearing gorgeous gowns of every color and the number of generals and high officials.

The dinner was lovely, and as the night went by, Lily Rose knew that while everyone was busy having after-dinner cocktails, it was now time for introductions to the key people she must somehow investigate. Alexander gently held her arm as he made his way across the room to General Nicolas Matias.

"General Matias!" spoke Alexander. "Pardon me, Sir, but I would like to introduce to you the lovely Maria Vasquez."

General Matias suddenly stopped his conversation with the two lovely ladies he had been talking to and turned his attention to Lily Rose. With a glass of brandy in hand, he quickly looked her up and down and smiled.

"Hello!" he nodded his head with approval. "Alexander, where did you find such a beauty as Miss Maria?" he asked with curiosity.

Alexander smiled and said, "Would you believe, General, we met at the beach earlier today? We had lunch together, and the rest is history."

They both smiled as General Matias said, "Maria, you must save me a dance."

Lily Rose smiled at him and said, "My pleasure, Sir!"

Then, Alexander quickly made his way through the room, introducing Lily Rose to many of the night's most influential people of Venezuela.

All through the night, Lily Rose danced with several of the

night's most influential elite; however, she saved the last dance for Alexander. She completed her homework by warming up to the several people who were on her list.

The next day and the months that followed, Lily Rose and Alexander spent nearly all their free time together. She was close now, and she knew it. Then, one day while lying on the beach, relaxing in the sun, Lily Rose saw Alexander watching her from the restaurant outside at the hotel. He soon turned his attention to the two men who joined him for lunch. She continued to watch as they were now in deep conversation with each other.

She quickly turned on her radio and pulled up the antenna. As it sat upon the white sand, she turned it to channel eighty-eight point five. It had crystal-clear reception. It was just one of the several tools given to her by the USMC for her mission.

She listened very intently now. Alexander and General Matias were deep in conversation. They argued over Alexander leaving for a new shipment of special guns. Not just any weapons, but specialized weapons that were only used by the United States Military. It was a step beyond their ordinary shipments of AR-15s and normal weaponry they had dealt with.

"It is a game changer!" spoke General Matias to Alexander.

Then, General Alfredo Hernandez chimed in on the conversation. "Alexander, this shipment will allow us all to retire early. It is worth millions."

They all shook hands. Alexander nodded in agreement, and they all shook hands again.

Chapter 4

The Rondeveau

That night, after Alexander had dropped off Lily Rose, she quickly went to work. She put on a pair of old jeans and a t-shirt, swept back her hair in a ponytail, and put on an old ball cap. With her secret watch on her wrist and a backpack full of spy things, she was off.

She pulled up at Alexander's place in a small, unmarked car. She was sure to park out of the way in a secluded area. She sat and waited for any signs of Alexander or anyone in his circle.

An hour went by, and there was nothing—no movement or anything at all. Then, suddenly, out of the corner of her eye, she saw Alexander and two other guys walking out the front door of his place. Lily Rose just sat and watched them as all three got into a Bentley. They quickly sped off as she stayed far behind and followed.

She pulled up three car lengths down from where Alexander parked and sat, watching as the three men made their way into the abandoned building. Then, another car quickly pulled up beside the Bentley. Out walked General Matias and General Hernandez. With the old building lit up, Lily Rose could see the men gathered, but she couldn't make out what was going on exactly. So, she turned on her recording device on her wrist and quickly grabbed her backpack.

She quietly made her way around the side of the building. She took a second look around her to make sure she wasn't followed. She placed a small, sticky device on the windowpane and pushed the reception button on her watch. She began to intercept their conversation.

As Lily Rose listened to the entire conversation about their plan to obtain a nuclear weapon from Iran, another car drove up. She quickly ducked her head and hid around the corner.

She couldn't believe her eyes! It was her longtime friend Gabriella's boyfriend, John Cruise. Lily Rose was shocked as her face quickly dropped. This was awful, she thought.

"I knew he was no good!" she said to herself.

She quietly turned and left. She knew enough. As she made her way back to her car, hidden down the road in a secluded location, Lily Rose felt she was being watched. She quickly got back into her car and left.

The next day, Lily Rose was enjoying her breakfast on the terrace of her hotel room when she heard a knock on her door. She peeked through the hole to see who it was, and to her surprise, it was a man with long brown hair to his shoulders and a well-groomed beard. She didn't recognize him until she looked into his eyes. She knew those piercing, deep-blue eyes from somewhere. Then it occurred to her... It was Captain Mark Spenser!

She slowly opened the door, and with her jaw dropped, he walked past her into her hotel room.

"What are you doing here, Captain Spenser?" she asked.

"Lily Rose!" he quickly snapped back. "You are going to compromise my whole mission."

Her face turned red with anger. She began to pace the floor now in her half-silk robe, which bared her long, tanned legs. Captain Spenser was amused now as he began to tighten his jaw. He found her completely intoxicating. As Lily Rose continued her argument, Captain Spenser found her irresistible. He imagined making love to her.

Then, as she noticed him staring at her in silence, Lily Rose realized that she only had a silk robe on. As she continued ranting, she simultaneously walked by her bed and put on an old pair of jeans. As she slid them on, Mark noticed the curve of her slender hips and long legs. It was more than he could stand. He quickly grabbed her and silenced her with a long, warm kiss. She hesitated at first, but quickly leaned into his kiss.

Chapter 5

Secrets and Lies

It was pouring rain, and Lily Rose and Mark Spenser were driving down the street in a black Mercedes when suddenly they both saw General Hernandez and General Matias being escorted from their limo into the big hotel. It was the same hotel where the big Gala had occurred only weeks before. Captain Spenser and Lily Rose quickly sprang into action.

Since it was the very same hotel where Lily Rose was registered as AKA Maria Vasquez, she ran upstairs to her room without being seen and changed into a stunning red dress, one that Chris De Luca could easily identify her in. As she made her way back downstairs, out of the corner of her eye, she saw her partner in a white waiter jacket approach her.

"Hello, beautiful!" he quickly said as he offered to walk her to her table. She smiled and walked behind him. He sat her across from the Generals' table.

As he began to take her order, General Matias had sent his personal assistant over to her table.

"Miss Vasquez! The General requests that you join him for lunch," said the assistant.

She quickly smiled and answered the man. "Tell the General that I would love to join him."

With that said, Maria Vasquez put on her game face and followed the man. With her secret earpiece in place, Lily Rose waited for help from her now partner, Captain Mark Spenser.

As the waiter left her table, he made his way into the back of the restaurant into an unoccupied room. He quickly told Lily Rose to pace herself and try to be natural, but to get as much information as she could about their next rendezvous.

Meanwhile, back at the table with the Generals, Lily Rose was quickly seated and joined their conversation.

"Hello, gentlemen!" said Maria Vasquez. "Thank you for inviting me to join you," she said as she quickly took her seat next to General Matias.

"My pleasure, Maria!" General Matias said as he placed his napkin in his lap. The waiter came over and quickly took their orders, as the Generals conversed. It was just a normal conversation about their families. It wasn't what Lily Rose had hoped for. Then, suddenly, General Matias turned to Maria and asked her if she was in Venezuela for business or pleasure.

Maria swallowed her bite of food and started to slightly choke when hearing the question. Then, just as quickly, she cleared her throat and firmly said, "PLEASURE!"

"I see!" said the General. "I wonder, though, if you would be interested in being my personal assistant."

Lily Rose didn't see this coming, but it played perfectly into her plans. General Matias and General Hernandez quickly glanced at each other as Alexander looked sternly at General Matias and said, "But General, she knows nothing about that sort of thing!" Alexander was trying to somehow protect Maria before she got too deeply involved.

Then, taking into consideration what Alexander had said, General Matias spoke to Maria once again. "What do you think, Maria?"

Just then, Lily Rose heard a voice saying, "NO! SAY NO!" It was Captain Mark Spenser talking through her earpiece that Maria was wearing. As Lily Rose ignored the voice, she quickly turned and addressed General Matias.

"It would be an honor, General."

Chapter 6
The Deal

With her new job as personal assistant to General Matias, Maria Vasquez quickly fell into routine, doing every odd and end job she was asked to do. She made all his travel plans, attended to his financial affairs, planned his daily routines, and even arranged his laundry service.

However, in between her busy day, she found time to slowly gather evidence against not only General Matias, but General Hernandez as well. In fact, Lily Rose gathered evidence that had even led back to the ringleader of the whole operation—Vladimir Punchenski of Russia, including President Fedorov.

The days seemed to turn into months very quickly. It started out as summer, and now it was October. AKA Mark Spenser, although he wasn't happy about Lily Rose's job title, seemed content as long as she was in no immediate harm. It was more than a job, and Captain Chris De Luca knew it. It was an assignment, and Lily Rose was one of the best he had seen. She had the right looks and skills to pull it off. She had now infiltrated their target. She was doing a great job—at least so far. But, deep inside his gut, he knew he had to keep a close watch on her. He was falling in love with her. She was his world now.

Captain De Luca knew he couldn't take any chances with anyone of their targets finding out her identity.

She came to him that night in a white silk robe. Her tanned skin glistened against it, and her long black hair swayed against her back as she walked toward him. She lightly licked her lips as she looked at him with hunger in her eyes. He took her gently in his arms and kissed her neck, then her ruby lips. Lily Rose kissed him back as she moaned. Captain De Luca laid her gently on the bed, and they made love all night.

Captain De Luca woke up longing for his love. He quickly got dressed and closed the door behind him. As he drove to Lily Rose's place, on his way, he saw a light on at the building of General Matias, where his business deals took place. He quickly pulled over and saw the silhouette of two people by the window. He got out of the car and ran up as quickly as he could, being careful not to be seen.

As Chris De Luca stood outside the door, he overheard two voices talking. It was Lily Rose and Alexander—General Matias's right-hand man. Captain De Luca whispered under his breath, "The little bastard! He always had a thing for Lily Rose." Then he heard Lily Rose sternly tell Alexander to back off. That was all Captain De Luca needed to hear. He quickly grabbed a nearby garbage can, complete with a mop and mop bucket. He put on his old man face and entered the room. He flipped the light on and grabbed a broom.

"Oh, excuse me!" he said in his old man voice. "I wasn't aware anyone was still here."

Then, in an angry voice, Alexander said, "Old man, go clean another room. You can see we are busy."

With that said, Lily Rose and Captain De Luca locked eyes. She knew those dark blue eyes anywhere. Then she said, "Excuse me, sir, but as you can see, I am quite busy."

"Yes! You heard the lady," said Alexander.

"Oh! Well, excuse me!" Captain De Luca quickly said. "I'm terribly sorry for disturbing you. I thought the lady was in distress."

He turned to leave, but not before emptying the trash can next to him. It had several papers of importance. As he walked out and down the hall, Captain De Luca heard a sudden thud and crash. "That's my girl!" he smiled and said. It appeared that Alexander did not take Lily Rose's request seriously. After he asked for another kiss, Lily Rose had had enough. She flipped him over and slammed him to the ground.

Inside his car now, Captain De Luca watched as Lily Rose came out, then he safely followed her home.

The next day, things had gotten complicated for Lily Rose. Alexander, bitter from the night's events and being rejected by Lily

Rose, had convinced General Matias that she was a spy. That morning, as soon as AKA Maria Vasquez arrived, General Matias had a surprise for her.

"Maria, I want you to cancel your plans for today and go with me on a trip."

Stunned, Maria looked at him with uncertainty. With a slight hesitance in her voice, she quickly said, "With your busy schedule and mine as well, are you sure, sir?"

Captain Matias looked at her sternly now and responded back, "I need your help on this important trip, Maria. So, go home and pack, and I'll send a limo within the hour to pick you up."

With that said, he quickly left.

Lily Rose quickly did as she was instructed. Before she left her apartment, she wrote a message for Captain De Luca and sent it by courier.

The limo arrived, and as she got in, Lily Rose had an uneasy feeling. Inside the limo were General Matias and Alexander. It was quiet, and Alexander seemed to have a slight smile on his face as he conversed quietly with the General.

The limo quickly pulled up to the private jet, and off they went, destination unknown.

Meanwhile, back at his hotel, Chris De Luca was busy

talking to his contacts about his next move. He suddenly heard a knock at the door. As he peeked through the peephole of the door, it was a courier on a bicycle. He quickly answered the door and took the letter. As he read the letter from Lily Rose, his jaw tightened, and he clenched his teeth.

"Damn! She's been kidnapped!"

Chapter 7

Bold and Beautiful

On the plane, looking out her window, Lily Rose had her thoughts interrupted by a glass of champagne that was offered to her.

"No, thank you," she said politely.

"But the General insists," Alexander replied.

As she took the champagne, she had a gut feeling not to drink it because it was laced with a drug. But, to keep the peace, she took a small sip.

"Good girl!" said General Matias as he sat in the seat next to her. "Alexander has informed me that you are a spy, Miss Vasquez," the General calmly said.

Lily Rose laughed out loud and then got angry. "Alexander is a liar and angry at me for not kissing him last night."

"Oh really?" the General said with a slight sarcastic tone.

"Yes," said Lily Rose.

With that said, Lily Rose drifted off to sleep. The drug-laced champagne had taken effect.

Captain De Luca and his team were ready in the Brazilian

jungle. They had intercepted the location of the plane with the General and Lily Rose.

After sleeping for several hours, Lily Rose woke up with the landing of the plane. She gently rubbed her eyes and winced at the slight headache she now had.

After they left the plane and began to enter the limo that was waiting for the General, Captain De Luca and his team began to fire on the General and his entourage.

The General, caring only for his own life, quickly jumped into the limo, and it sped off.

On the ground, face down, Lily Rose hid behind a baggage cart. She peeked around the corner to see if it was clear to make a mad dash but was quickly surrounded by Captain De Luca and his team.

Lily Rose quickly jumped into his arms. After only a few minutes, as she calmed down, Lily Rose suddenly slapped Captain De Luca square in the face. He was surprised by her sudden change.

As he grabbed her by the arm, he said, "So much for saving your life!"

As Lily Rose began to argue, Captain De Luca quickly put her in the back of the military jeep before she could utter a word.

As they sped off down the road, Lily Rose asked, "Where

are we going?"

"To the jungle, my love."

"This is not over yet! We've got to catch the General and stop the arms trade before the Russians leave the country."

Chapter 8

Bold and Beautiful

Standing now in the middle of the Brazilian jungle, Lily-Rose and Captain DeLuca started to argue. Lily-Rose wanted to go after the General too, but Captain DeLuca wanted her to stay safe. As they continued to argue, the earth suddenly gave way. Down the steep hill they went. It was a mudslide. As they plunged down the slippery slope, hitting the thick, green foliage along the way, they flew mid-air and landed in a pool of blue water.

Captain DeLuca yelled to his men up above the cliff to continue to the nearest city. "We will meet you there," he said.

As they began to swim to the shore, it suddenly began to thunder. In front of them was a cave. They both ran out of the rain, and the Captain quickly built a fire to warm them. As they warmed themselves up by the fire, they looked at each other and began to laugh. As the flames of the fire lit up the cave, Lily-Rose noticed from the corner of her eye, writing on the cave wall. She told the Captain, "It is very old."

He asked her, "How do you know this?"

She replied, "Because I studied ancient archaeology."

He looked at her with amazement as he said, "I never knew."

She replied, "Captain DeLuca, there are many things about me that you don't know."

She looked at him and smiled.

Lily-Rose quickly turned her attention back to the wall and the writing. As she read the writing and examined the drawings on the wall, it occurred to her that it was some kind of lost treasure. Then, suddenly, it came to her. She quickly yelled at Captain DeLuca, "It's the lost map treasure of Dom Pedro!"

"Who?" he said.

Lily-Rose turned to Captain DeLuca and started to explain, "Dom Pedro was the eighteenth-century emperor of Spain. When his empire was in jeopardy, he escaped to Brazil and set up his empire here," she said. "It's legendary!" Lily-Rose said.

As Captain DeLuca examined the wall closer now, he said with curiosity, "Really! Where is the treasure?"

He asked, "Does the map show where?"

As Lily-Rose examined the map, she said, "It's under two waterfalls."

They both just looked at each other now and grinned.

As they sat down by the fire again to warm themselves, Captain DeLuca noticed her tanned skin, glowing by the fire. "Lily-Rose, I have to admit," he said. "You are a very beautiful woman and an incredible one as well."

Their eyes quickly met, as he reached in to kiss her soft, warm lips. Lily-Rose didn't hesitate. She reached in for his kiss and suddenly realized that this is where she was meant to be—in the arms of the man of her dreams. As the glow of the embers kissed their skin, they made love all night.

The following day, after leaving the cave, they started to make their way to the closest city. As they made their way through the jungle, they searched for the two waterfalls. After walking through the treacherous jungle for miles, it was now midday. They stopped to rest at a nearby spring to refresh themselves. As they drank their fill, they shared a wet kiss.

Suddenly, laughter rang out behind them. As they both turned to see, they saw that it was a group of village children laughing at the two lovers as they shared their kiss. Then, just as quickly as they appeared, the children were gone. A jeep suddenly pulled up. Out of the Jeep Renegade stood a short man, dressed in jungle attire, complete with both hat and camping gear. "Hello! I'm Jerry T. Jackson, tour guide of these parts."

He was a peculiar little man, as he rambled on and on about his accomplishments. Lily-Rose smiled to herself, thinking he was funny, yet slightly odd. He seemed too nervous to be a tour guide, she thought. Just then, Captain DeLuca introduced himself and Lily-

Rose to Mr. Jackson as they shook hands.

"Would you happen to know the location of two waterfalls?" Captain DeLuca asked Mr. Jackson.

"Yes! Of course," Mr. Jackson replied. "Turn around and to your left," he said.

As they all proceeded to turn around, Mr. Jackson said, "Now look over there behind that rock that looks like a face. Right behind it are the two waterfalls."

Then, suddenly, they heard gunfire. They were all being shot at by a strange group of men. They quickly jumped into the jeep and took off as fast as they could.

With Mr. Jackson behind the wheel of the Jeep Renegade, they sped through the shallow creek. However, unknown to them all, there was deep water just ahead of them. Within minutes, the jeep filled with water.

"Jump!" said Captain DeLuca.

As they jumped into the blue water and began to swim, gunfire rang in the air. They were being shot at by a group of men from the shore. Just then, a tree log came floating by. They all three grabbed on quickly, as it carried them to the other side of the river, near the twin waterfalls. They fell on the beach and caught their breath.

Mr. Jackson suddenly said, in between gasps of air and without hesitation, "Who was shooting at us?"

"I didn't sign up for this!"

"This is not in my job description!"

They all got to their feet, but as they did, they began to hear singing. It was the beautiful voice of a little girl. Mr. Jackson continued his rambling, but Lily-Rose quickly put her hand up to silence him. They all began to smile as the beautiful, angelic music seemed to get louder. As they followed the sound of the music, it took them underneath the two waterfalls. To their amazement, it was a cave. With each step they took, the singing was more intense.

"Are you guys sure we should continue?" Mr. Jackson said with a slight quiver in his voice. "I mean, maybe we should go have a drink at a bar or something!" he said.

But onward they continued. Suddenly, appearing before their eyes, was a glowing, white light and a beautiful girl sitting on a small throne, that seemed to be made just for her. She had an angelic fair complexion and shoulder-length brown hair that seemed to shine in the white light surrounding her.

She suddenly stopped singing when she saw the guests. "Who are you?" she asked gently.

Lily-Rose quickly spoke up, "I am Lily-Rose, and these two

gentlemen are Mr. Jackson and Captain DeLuca."

"Why are you here?" the little girl asked.

"We are searching for the lost treasure of Dom Pedro," Lily-Rose said.

As the little girl's brown eyes began to twinkle, she batted her long lashes and said, "Step forward, please. Behind me is a secret wall. It contains the treasure of Dom Pedro. However, once you bring me the golden egg of Dom Pedro, that was stolen many years ago by General Matias, the treasure will be yours."

Lily-Rose looked at Captain DeLuca with wide eyes now. "The golden egg is not to be trifled with!" the girl said. "It has great powers, from the ancient family line of Dom Pedro, and must be found! If its great powers are unleashed by the wrong hands, evil will follow," the little girl said in a desperate tone.

Suddenly, Mr. Jackson spoke up. "Who is General Matias?"

"He is a very evil man," said Lily-Rose.

"So, let me get this straight!" said Mr. Jackson. "To get this treasure, we've got to find and defeat an evil General, find a golden egg, and bring the egg back here to get this treasure?"

With his face flustered now, Mr. Jackson continued, "I did not sign up for no evil generals or powerful golden eggs! I'm just a tour guide," he said in a nervous tone.

Then, the little girl who sat on the throne said, "Make your way through the tunnel. At the end is a bridge to the city of Santa Catarina, where your journey will begin."

After they told the little girl goodbye, they made their way through the tunnel. Cobwebs lined the way. After what seemed like an hour, they reached the end of the eerie tunnel. There was a lever attached to a strange-looking board. After Captain DeLuca pulled the lever, the door suddenly opened.

Chapter 9
Count Down

With all the time spent inside the cave, day had now become night. As the moon shone brightly in the night sky, before them was a long bridge. It was made of rope and old planks of board. Although long, it was narrow in width.

"Don't look down!" said Captain DeLuca. Below the bridge was a river several hundred feet down.

As they began to make their way across the eerie-looking bridge, with each step, it swayed slightly. Mr. Jackson winced and began to cry. In a trembling voice, he said, "God! From now on, I'm going to be a good person. I know I shouldn't have taken that jeep without permission." With that said, they continued to make their way across the creaky, old bridge. Suddenly, Mr. Jackson's foot fell through one of the old planks.

"Help!" he cried out, as he clung for dear life to the nearby rope. Quickly, Captain DeLuca grabbed onto Mr. Jackson's arm and pulled him back onto the bridge. Mr. Jackson, with eyes wide with fear, was profusely sweating now. They quickly continued over the bridge as Mr. Jackson continued his conversation with God all the way. After finally making it to the other side of the bridge, they heard music ringing in the air. Before them was the village of Santa

Catarina.

After making their way through the lush, thick forest, they finally arrived at the village. Music played loudly as the villagers danced in the street. Colorful costumes adorned them, and flags of their country flew in the night air. With so many people crowding the street, the three were quickly swept into a little shop. The lady of the shop quickly came forward.

"I am Selina," she said politely. The lady of the shop was dressed in a yellow and red skirt and matching top, with a beautiful headdress to match. "Please feel free to find yourself a costume to wear for the celebration," she said.

After they all had found a new change of clothes to wear, Selina said, "That will be five hundred American dollars." Captain DeLuca's jaw tightened, and his face dropped, but he paid the lady what they owed her.

Back in the crowded streets now, Mr. Jackson smiled and said, "I'll be over there at that bar." With that, he was gone. Alone now, Lily-Rose and Captain DeLuca had their own adult beverages as they continued to make their way down the street. As the people continued to dance and enjoy the music and festivities all around them, Lily-Rose started to feel the effects of her drink now. She smiled and looked at Captain DeLuca as she said, "Would you dance with me, Captain DeLuca?"

He flashed her a smile as he looked at her. He noticed her tanned skin against the bright yellow dress that clung tightly to her body. It was cut low at her breast and up the side, showing her long, tanned leg.

"I would love to," he said. As they danced to the music, Lily-Rose swayed gently in his arms. Her breasts gently caressed his chest as Captain DeLuca's jaw tightened. He looked at her intensely now.

Later that night, as the festivities came to an end, Captain DeLuca found them a little bungalow for the night. The room was small, but it was nice. As Lily-Rose stepped closer to the window, the moonlight swept over her body. Captain DeLuca's eyes swept over her body. He smiled to himself and knew with certainty at that moment that he was in love with her. He boldly took her in his arms and slowly undressed her. They made love through the night.

The next morning, the sun shone brightly through the window. As Lily-Rose began to wake up, she grabbed her aching head and slightly moaned. Just then, Captain DeLuca walked through the door with breakfast.

"Good morning, beautiful!" he said with a smile.

As she wiped the sleep from her eyes, she sipped her coffee and began to dress. Suddenly, they heard a loud commotion outside the window. Several military jeeps had pulled up to the building.

Captain DeLuca quickly grabbed Lily-Rose by the arm as they ran toward the back of the building.

They quickly made their way down a winding staircase and ran out the door. They jumped into the closest car and sped down the road. There was a tiki hut just before them. Mr. Jackson lay on top of it, sleeping. He was a small man, dressed in a grass skirt. Hearing the car pull up, Mr. Jackson quickly sat up.

"Hey, you!" said Captain DeLuca to Mr. Jackson. "Get in!" he said.

Dressed only in a grass skirt, with no shirt or shoes, Mr. Jackson quickly jumped in. Shots began to ring in the air. The Brazilian Militia began firing on the small car as it made its way down the dirt road that led into the forest.

Suddenly, a long, black car pulled up at the small building where the army jeeps were. Out of the car stood General Matias.

"Where are they?" he said in a deep, authoritative voice.

The soldier next to the General quickly spoke. "They escaped out the back of the building, General." General Matias slammed his fist into the side of the soldier's jaw, and he fell to the ground.

"We must find them!" the general said angrily.

Meanwhile, Captain DeLuca continued driving the car

through the forest on the dirt road. They had finally come to a river. As they all three looked out their window, they saw a camp just on the other side of the river.

"It looks like my men!" said Captain DeLuca. Captain DeLuca's man in charge quickly approached the car. He smiled as he saw how Captain DeLuca was dressed.

"What are you smiling at?" Captain DeLuca said in a stern voice.

"I do apologize, Captain, but you look like a villager in your red pants and yellow shirt." Captain DeLuca quickly dismissed what his man in charge had said as he asked for a clean uniform.

"Make those two uniforms!" said Captain DeLuca, as he quickly turned and looked at Mr. Jackson, who was wearing his grass skirt.

Later that day, after Captain DeLuca was back in full uniform and they had eaten their fill, Lily-Rose asked the Captain, "So, what is our next move?"

"You, my dear, are staying here!" he said in a stern voice.

Lily-Rose looked up at him with narrowed eyes. The anger began to build now. Suddenly, in an angry voice, she said, "I don't think so! You forget your place, Mr. DeLuca!" she said sternly. "I am a trained professional, and I can take care of myself," she said with assurance.

Captain DeLuca smiled slightly, as he thought to himself. "You are right, my dear. I forgot just how well trained you are. But you must stay close beside me," he said sternly.

"We are going to the headquarters of General Matias," he said quickly. "Operations has instructed us to take down the arms trade deal planned for tonight between General Matias and the Russians," he concluded.

Just then, Mr. Jackson's eyes widened in surprise. He quickly said, "No, thank you!" he said. "I think I like the grass skirt and tiki hut better."

Then, Captain DeLuca interrupted as he said, "Mr. Jackson, they know who you are now!" he said matter-of-factly. "I'm afraid that you must go as well for your own safety," he said.

They quickly planned for their operation and set off for the General.

Chapter 10

The Secret Operation

It was three in the morning on a clear night. The two generals sat in the long black limo discussing their plans as a jeep and three big trucks pulled up alongside them on the tarmac. It was John Cruise. He had delivered the shipment of illegal arms as promised. As the three men finalized the deal, Vladimir Punchenski's plane was landing on the airstrip. He was the go-between for the arms deal for President Federov of Russia.

As the men gathered in front of the three big trucks loaded with the shipment of illegal arms, they began to laugh at their wicked plan. Vladimir Punchenski held the suitcase of money and quickly opened it up, displaying the five-hundred million as promised. Suddenly, the tarps on the three trucks swung open, with federal agents appearing as several federal helicopters swooped down on the tarmac.

John Cruise had not realized that his secret operation had been carefully watched for months. As gunfire rang out in the night sky between the Bazillion army and the Feds, the two generals and Vladimir Punchenski quickly escaped in the limo.

In hot pursuit of the limo was Captain DeLuca and his men. After several minutes, the limo made it to the underground compound that was waiting for the generals. Captain DeLuca and his men quickly swooped down on the compound and surrounded it. But little did the Feds know that behind the secret wall of General Matias's library was a cave that led to his private plane.

As Captain DeLuca and the Feds made their way into the compound, sitting inside the chopper waiting were Lily-Rose and Mr. Jackson. Captain DeLuca had made them both wait. Although Lily-Rose was reluctant, she agreed.

Lily-Rose and Mr. Jackson sat alone in the helicopter. Suddenly, in an angry tone, Lily-Rose said, "If he thinks I'm going to just sit here, he is crazy!"

With that said, Lily-Rose made her way out of the helicopter.

"Wait!" said Mr. Jackson. "I'm coming too! I mean, who is going to protect you?"

Lily-Rose smiled as she remembered how afraid Mr. Jackson had been crossing the bridge only a few days ago.

"Come on then!" she said without hesitation.

The federal agents continued to invade the compound as Lily-Rose and Mr. Jackson quickly made their way around the back of the building. The sun was going down fast now as the night sky was quickly taking its place. Lily-Rose saw a window that was slightly open. She turned back to Mr. Jackson and said, "Let me give you a boost up. And then you pull me through! OK?"

However, after boosting up Mr. Jackson, his short legs got stuck in the window.

"Help! Help me!" said Mr. Jackson in a panic.

"Be quiet!" said Lily-Rose. "They will hear you," she said sternly.

With that said, Mr. Jackson suddenly crashed to the floor beneath him. As he made his way back to his feet, he mumbled something under his breath. He quickly took Lily-Rose by the hand and lifted her up through the window.

"We must be in the basement of the compound," she said.

The walls were eerie and filled with cobwebs. Suddenly, a mouse scurried across the floor.

"Oh my goodness!" Mr. Jackson said as he jumped in fright.

As they continued on, it occurred to Lily-Rose that they could hear no sounds from the compound above them.

"It must be soundproof," she said.

Directly in front of them now was a door. She slowly opened it, and they heard voices from across the room. There was a small plane, and the men were just on the other side of the plane.

"It's the generals and Vladimir Punchenski," she whispered

to Mr. Jackson.

Quickly, Lily-Rose and Mr. Jackson made their way behind the plane so they could hear more clearly.

"We must go to plan B!" said General Hernandez sternly. "Dom Pedro's Treasure," he said.

The shock of what they both had just heard was evident in both Lily-Rose and Mr. Jackson's eyes now. Then suddenly, Mr. Jackson sneezed. The three men jumped in surprise.

"Behind the plane!" said General Matias.

Vladimir Punchenski quickly grabbed them both.

"Good! We have hostages now!" said General Hernandez.

Chapter 11

Hostage Situation

They were both blindfolded and seated in chairs beside the three men, but not without a struggle from Lily-Rose. Vladimir Punchenski had to make her see things his way. He pulled out his handgun and pointed it directly at her before she finally gave in to their evil scheme.

Meanwhile, inside the compound, Captain De Luca found a hidden door just behind the bookshelf. He quickly opened the door, and his agents moved in. When Captain De Luca saw Lily-Rose blindfolded, his heart sank. "Damn her!" he muttered to himself.

With raised guns, the agents began to close in. Vladimir quickly grabbed Lily-Rose and held her at gunpoint.

"You are surrounded!" Captain De Luca shouted.

In his thick Russian accent, Vladimir replied firmly, "I'm in control here now."

"We are getting on the plane now!" he added.

With that, both generals boarded the plane. As the tense exchange of words continued between Captain De Luca and Vladimir, Lily-Rose knew she had to act. She remembered the teachings of her Sensei. Still blindfolded, Lily-Rose took control.

Before anyone could react, she performed a turn-around flip, seized Vladimir's gun, and quickly removed her blindfold, now holding him at gunpoint.

Just then, the small plane began to take off. Captain De Luca ran toward Lily-Rose and seized Vladimir Punchenski. The agents opened fire on the small plane, but it was too far gone. As soon as the agents took Vladimir into custody, Captain De Luca pulled Lily-Rose into his arms and held her tightly against his chest.

After a moment, he released her and planted a firm kiss on her lips. "Don't ever do this to me again!" he scolded, letting out a relieved sigh.

Across the room, Mr. Jackson cleared his throat and said, "Hello! Did you forget about me?" He was still sitting in the chair, blindfolded. Lily-Rose and Captain De Luca laughed as they untied his blindfold.

As they all began to leave the room, Mr. Jackson noticed something on the floor. "Look!" he said, pointing to an object lying outside the bag, near where the plane had been sitting. "They must have dropped it!"

Lily-Rose approached it first. "It's shiny," she said.

Captain De Luca quickly retrieved the brown sack. As he pulled the object from the bag and read the inscription on the golden statue, he smiled and said, "Looks like we've found the statue of Dom Pedro's Treasure."

Chapter 12

The Search for Dom Pedro's Treasure

Later that night, after everyone had settled down, Lily-Rose, Captain De Luca, and Mr. Jackson sat by the fire. As they celebrated a successful mission, they shared a drink. She held the golden statue in her hands and examined it more closely. She found an inscription on the side in small letters.

"Look!" she said. "There is an inscription on the side of it. It's in Spanish!" She began to read it slowly. "Through the mist as the sun sets, the secret lies beneath the rainbow!"

In unison, they all three said, "HUH?"

Mr. Jackson said with a sarcastic tone, "Here we go again!"

With that, the next morning, they set off for Dom Pedro's treasure.

Packed and ready for their trip through the Amazon Forest, they began their journey on foot. The forest was thick and lush with a variety of exotic plants and a beautiful array of birds. A map reader of old antiquities, Lily-Rose directed the way. Captain De Luca led them through the forest with a large blade in hand, cutting a path as they walked. With mosquitoes and bugs buzzing all around them now, Mr. Jackson busied himself by spraying mosquito spray in the air and over them.

"These mosquitoes are as big as dragonflies!" he said matter-of-factly.

After a few miles of walking, the sun began to go down fast. Captain De Luca decided it was best to set up camp near the river in a clear location.

After eating their fill, they all sat beside the campfire discussing their plans for the next day. Suddenly, a long snake appeared next to Mr. Jackson from the trees above.

"Don't move, Mr. Jackson!" said Captain De Luca sternly. Mr. Jackson's eyes were wide with fright.

Captain De Luca calmly picked up his handgun and shot the snake dead. The large snake fell to the ground. Instantly, Mr. Jackson jumped up and began to twist and shout in disgust.

"UUUUGH! No way!" he said in anguish.

Lily-Rose quickly calmed him down. "It will be okay, Mr. Jackson! Here, have a sip of whiskey to calm your nerves!" she said firmly.

A few minutes later, Lily-Rose turned in for the night as she began to yawn. Mr. Jackson decided he would go to sleep as well, but not before picking up a large stick for his protection. Captain De Luca continued to sit by the campfire and sip more whiskey. He quickly stoked the fire as he kept the first watch.

A few hours later, Lily-Rose kept watch to give the captain his rest. Captain De Luca laid his head on his makeshift pillow and slept with one eye open.

Chapter 13
The Search Continues

The next day, as the three continued onward through the Amazon, they suddenly heard a loud noise from the forest. With his gun in hand, Captain De Luca made Lily-Rose and Mr. Jackson stand behind him for their own protection. A flock of beautiful birds then flew from the tree above them. Out of nowhere, a big black panther suddenly dropped in front of them. It growled at them, showing its large fangs. They were paralyzed with fear.

Slowly, Captain De Luca raised his gun and shot several rounds into the air. The panther quickly scurried off.

"Oh my!" said Mr. Jackson. "I'm not sure I like any of this," he said with a slight quiver in his voice. "This forest has some scary critters in it!" he continued, walking behind the others.

Several hours later, as the sun began to go down, a mist started to form in the air above the river they had been following. Just a mile down the river, a double rainbow appeared in the sky. Just below the rainbow was a beautiful waterfall.

"It's a clue!" said Lily-Rose. Now, they had to figure out how to cross the river to reach the waterfall.

They each looked around to find something to cross the

river. A few minutes later, Captain De Luca yelled out, "I found something!" The other two quickly ran to where he was. It was a makeshift raft made from old planks of wood. Captain De Luca jumped up and down on it momentarily to test if it was safe enough to cross.

After only a few minutes, they had crossed the river and gotten off the raft. Making their way toward the waterfall, they continued looking for another clue. As they walked, each going their own way, Lily-Rose came across some tall green plants next to a cave. As she entered the cave, she yelled at the others.

Examining the walls of the cave with a flashlight in hand, the two men came running up beside her. There were ancient drawings on the cave wall before them.

"It's another clue!" said Lily-Rose.

"Shall we continue?" asked Captain De Luca. Once again, he led the way as they continued their search for Dom Pedro's treasure.

After walking for what seemed like an hour or more, they heard a noise just behind them. Captain De Luca and Lily-Rose suspected that someone was following them now. The captain pulled out his gun as he continued to lead them through the twisting, winding cave.

They momentarily stopped so Lily-Rose could examine the golden statue again. As Mr. Jackson took a step backward, he stumbled over a small boulder. He fell into Lily-Rose, and they both crashed down—along with the golden statue. Looking at the broken pieces of the statue, Lily-Rose cried out, "No!"

Picking up the broken pieces, Lily-Rose came across a bigger piece. After picking it up, she found a golden key underneath it.

"What does this go to?" she asked in surprise.

"It is apparently another clue," said Captain De Luca.

"I was just going to say how sorry I was," said Mr. Jackson. "But this is a good thing, right?" he said with uncertainty.

Chapter 15
Danger Lurks

With the golden key in hand, they continued onward. The sounds of footsteps seemed to get louder. Suddenly, gunfire rang out, and several men appeared before them. It was General Hernandez and his men.

"Hello!" he said. "So we meet again."

"I purposely left the bag next to the plane," he continued. "I knew you would lead us to the treasure," he added with certainty.

"How did you escape?" asked Captain De Luca.

"It was easy," said General Hernandez. "You see, I have people on the inside of the federal agency working for me," he said matter-of-factly.

Captain De Luca tightened his jaw, smiling to himself now, wondering who the traitor, or traitors, in the agency were.

"I suggest you throw your gun to me, Captain De Luca," said the general.

With five guns pointing at him, Captain De Luca did not resist. He did as he was told and threw his gun over to the general.

"I know you didn't know this, but I am the great-grandson

of Dom Pedro," said General Hernandez. "So you see, the treasure is mine," he said self-assuredly. "I've been trying to locate his treasure for years now," he added. "However, I didn't realize the statue held a golden key," he explained.

"Continue on, but no tricks! Or I won't hesitate to shoot you!" the general said firmly.

With that, they all continued onward. After another thirty minutes, Lily-Rose exclaimed, "Look! Here's a knob on the wall, and it has a keyhole in it!" She smiled and inserted the golden key. The door opened before them.

They all walked through the opened door. Captain De Luca saw a torch on the wall and quickly lit it. Also on the wall was a trough filled with oil. He lit it as well. The fire that filled the trough blazed all around the room.

With the room completely lit, the room glowed from the embers of the fire. However, it was not the only thing that filled the room. Before them was the lost treasure of Dom Pedro. Their eyes all widened in amazement at the beautiful sight.

Chapter 16

The Power of Dom Pedro

With guns still pointing at Lily-Rose, Captain De Luca, and Mr. Jackson, General Hernandez instructed his men to tie the three prisoners up.

"The treasure is my legacy!" General Hernandez said with a smile.

Mr. Jackson carelessly tripped over his own feet as he backed up from the soldier. He fell upon a lever protruding from the wall. Instantly, an eerie breeze flowed through the room. Then, it became strangely quiet. Suddenly, the room was filled with the ghost of Dom Pedro, who had protected the treasure. General Hernandez and his men shrieked in utter fright.

Captain De Luca quickly grabbed Lily-Rose and Mr. Jackson, instructing them to hide their faces in the corner. He covered them all with his arm as the ghost of Dom Pedro unleashed his power. The power of Dom Pedro consumed the room, quickly sucking the life from General Hernandez and his men.

In only a matter of minutes, it was over. Captain De Luca and Lily-Rose slowly uncovered their faces and looked around. With the cave still lit and the treasure still in place, the ghost was gone. Mr. Jackson was still crouched down, his face covered. He was shaking in sheer fright. Lily-Rose gently touched his shoulder, and he screamed.

"Mr. Jackson?" she gently said. "It's over. You can uncover your face."

Mr. Jackson slowly uncovered his face as he stood up. With his knees still shaking, he said, "I think I need some clean pants now."

Lily-Rose and Captain De Luca smiled at each other as they embraced.

As the room glowed from the fire that lit the room and Dom Pedro's treasure, all three just stared around the room. Suddenly, before their eyes appeared the little princess from the cave of their last adventure.

"You have successfully rid Dom Pedro's treasure of the evil guardian. It is now yours to have," the princess said. "Now, I can finally take my rest."

With that said, the princess vanished.

"It's ours?" yelled Mr. Jackson with excitement. "Ha! Ha! Yes! It's ours!"

Then, Captain De Luca spoke up. "It rightfully belongs to the people of Brazil," he said. "Preferably in a museum, where everyone can enjoy its history."

With that said, Mr. Jackson's face fell. "We can't even have a gold bar?" he asked.

"Maybe just one or two," Captain De Luca said with a smile. "I'm sure they won't miss a few of them."

Mr. Jackson smiled once again. Lily-Rose and Captain De Luca embraced and kissed.

"Get a room!" said Mr. Jackson.

Chapter 17

The Tropics

Lily-Rose sat in her beach chair on a white sandy beach with a drink in her hand. Looking straight ahead, she saw Captain De Luca coming out of the ocean from his swim. Drying himself off, he bent over to kiss Lily-Rose.

"Hello, my dear!" he said.

"You know, Captain, it's a good thing we knew each other before we became filthy rich," she said with a smile.

He kissed her again, but this time much deeper.

"You are right, my love," he replied.

Meanwhile, Mr. Jackson enjoyed himself as he drove down a busy street in Miami in his new sports car.

Chapter 18

One Year Later

It was one year later, and busy training for their next mission at the federal facility were Lily-Rose and Captain De Luca. The two were in the training rink, showing their new recruits karate techniques.

In a sarcastic but fun tone, Captain De Luca told Lily-Rose, "I'll try and take it easy on you." Then he smiled to himself.

Lily-Rose was infuriated now. Her cheeks grew hot from her anger. She quickly spun around and kicked the Captain square in the jaw. He quickly fell to his knees as Lily-Rose smiled to herself.

Before things could get too heated between them, a messenger from the agency's Secretary General's office of the Ministry interrupted them.

"Excuse me!" he said. "I have an urgent message for you both. You are both to report to the Secretary's office immediately!" The messenger said.

Chapter 19

New Assignment

Standing in the Secretary's office now were Lily-Rose and Captain De Luca. The Secretary, sitting in his leather chair at his desk, was a balding man. Dressed in his black suit with his tie loosened, he addressed his two agents who stood before him.

"You both were so successful on your last mission that I want you both on this next assignment," he said without hesitation.

Captain De Luca was not amused, as he did not want Lily-Rose on another dangerous mission. However, Lily-Rose was highly trained. She smiled to herself now with anticipation.

"Your next assignment is in Geneva, Switzerland," the Secretary said. "There is illegal trading going on there, within a secret organization. The man in charge is Liam Andros. He is very dangerous and not to be trifled with. You must find a way to infiltrate the organization and bring Liam Andros down."

Before Captain De Luca or Lily-Rose could say anything, the Secretary cleared his throat and continued, "There is also something else." He quickly said, "The missing Chalice of Louis XVI has gone missing. It is priceless!" He said sternly.

Chapter 20
Ready! Set! Go!

Sipping a glass of wine in front of the fireplace now were Captain De Luca and Lily-Rose. The crackling of the fire echoed as the embers burned brightly. Captain De Luca and Lily-Rose embraced as she leaned into his warm kiss.

Tomorrow, their new adventure would begin…